D0177548

To Miss Choppy Waters,
for her kind assistance

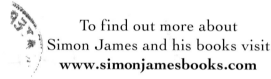

To find out more about
Simon James and his books visit
www.simonjamesbooks.com

First published 2007 by Walker Books Ltd
87 Vauxhall Walk, London SE11 5HJ

2 4 6 8 10 9 7 5 3 1

© 2007 Simon James

The right of Simon James to be identified as author/illustrator
of this work has been asserted by him in accordance with the
Copyright, Designs and Patents Act 1988

This book has been typeset in Cochin

Printed in China

British Library Cataloguing in Publication Data:
a catalogue record for this book is
available from the British Library

ISBN 978-1-4063-0240-0

www.walkerbooks.co.uk

Baby
Brains
and
ROBOMUM

Simon James

WALKER BOOKS
AND SUBSIDIARIES
LONDON • BOSTON • SYDNEY • AUCKLAND

Before Baby Brains was born, Mrs Brains ate lots of fish and lots of nuts, which are good for brains.

She also played foreign languages on headphones and read out loud to the baby inside her tummy. Mr and Mrs Brains were hoping for a clever baby.

But when Baby Brains was born, they were amazed to see just how clever he turned out to be.

When the hospital scanned Baby Brains's brain, they compared it with a normal baby's brain and ...

they were amazed
at the results!

At home, Baby Brains
had no time for toys.
He preferred working
on the computer

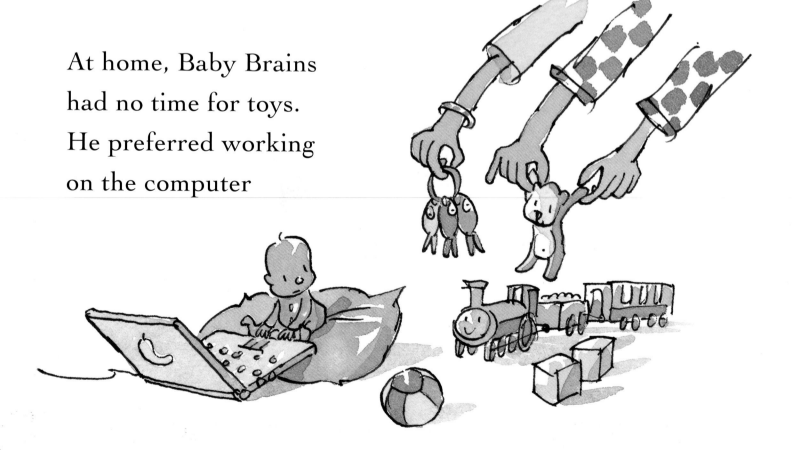

and doing experiments with his chemistry set.

But most of all, he loved to design new inventions.

Baby Brains invented
the first remote-controlled
self-rocking cradle.

He also invented the first
fully motorized baby buggy.

But despite his quite brilliant labour-saving inventions, Baby Brains couldn't fail to notice how tired his parents were at the end of each day.

Sometimes they were even too tired to read him a goodnight story.

One night, Baby Brains stayed up inventing something
special to help Mr and Mrs Brains.

He was sure science and technology would have the answer.
It took him all night and well into the next morning.

Finally, at lunchtime, he was able to present Mrs Brains with his most ambitious invention to date.

"It's RoboMum,"
said Baby Brains.
"Gosh!" said Mrs Brains.
"What does she do?"

"The ironing, for a start!" said Baby Brains.

"Fantastic!" said Mrs Brains.

RoboMum soon took over all the household chores.
She cooked the evening meal and washed up afterwards.

"Wonderful!" said
Mrs Brains.

The following day RoboMum had learnt to wash the car.
"Crikey!" said Mr Brains.

By the weekend RoboMum had taken over looking after the baby.

First she changed Baby Brains's nappy, but Baby Brains preferred his mum to do that.

Later she gave Baby Brains a bath, but Baby Brains preferred his dad to do that.

Worse was to come when RoboMum insisted on putting Baby Brains to bed. "Don't let the RoboBugs bite," said RoboMum.

"She's doing too much," said Mrs Brains. "And what's all that smoke coming out of her head?" said Mr Brains.

The next morning, instead of cereal, RoboMum served
nuts and bolts in engine oil for breakfast.
"Something is wrong," said Mr Brains.
"I think I'll have a yoghurt," said Mrs Brains.

Later RoboMum
washed Baby Brains
in the kitchen
sink with all
the dishes

and hung him out to dry on the line!

Baby Brains tried
to wriggle free,
but the pegs
held him in place.

He started to
sway in the breeze
along with all the
washing.

Baby Brains
began to cry.
"I want my mummy!"
he called.

Mrs Brains was upstairs when she heard her baby calling.
She looked out of the window and could hardly believe her eyes.

She raced
down the stairs,
through the kitchen

and into the garden.
She grabbed hold of her baby.

"Quick, Mum!"
said Baby Brains.
"I think
RoboMum is
about to ...

EXPLODE!"

As the smoke cleared, Mrs Brains held her baby tightly.
"Thanks, Mum," said Baby Brains.

That night, everyone helped cook dinner
and wash up afterwards.

Later Mr and Mrs Brains put Baby Brains to bed.
It was nice to do things together again.

Of course,
Baby Brains didn't stop inventing.

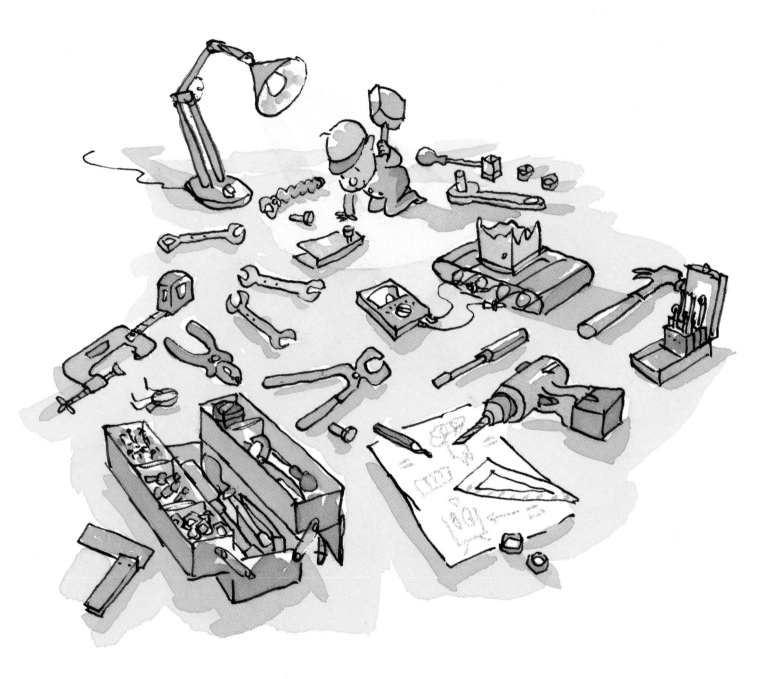

Soon he came up with something he was sure
his mum and dad would enjoy.
It was the new, improved ...

RoboMum 2!

The End